For my brothers and sisters—
Jamie, Jessica, Lauren, and Brian
—E.T.

To Nadia, who loves my
messes, colors, and surprises
—D.F.

A division of Bonnier Publishing
853 Broadway, New York, New York 10003
Text copyright ©2016 by Eric Telchin
Illustrations copyright © 2016 by Bonnier Publishing

Manufactured in China   LEO 0216
First Edition
2 4 6 8 10 9 7 5 3 1
Library of Congress Cataloging-in-Publication Data
is available upon request.
ISBN 978-1-4998-0277-1

littlebeebooks.com
bonnierpublishing.com

THE BLACK AND WHITE FACTORY

by ERIC TELCHIN   ILLUSTRATED by DIEGO FUNCK

little bee books

BLACK AND WHITE FACTO
Hello. And congratulations! You've just won a tour of the top-secret Black and White Factory.
Everything we make here is black and white. Checkerboards, dice, tuxedos... Even *we* are black and white!

*By turning the page, I, the reader of this book, solemnly swear to follow the factory rules. I will not make a mess. I will not bring colors into the factory. I will not initiate or participate in any surprises.

PLAYING CARDS
EIGHT BALLS
SALT & PEPPER
CHESS PIECES
TUXEDOS
TOP-SELLING BLACK AND WHITE PRODUCTS
TOP SECRET
EXPERIMENT ROOM
1 2
3 4
5 6
7 8
OPEN
Now let's take a peek inside the top-secret Experiment Room.

Welcome to the Bar Code Room—the cleanest, most perfect, most black and white room in the whole factory. Every bar code in the world is made right here. Even *this* book has one! Turn the book over to the back cover and see for yourself!
O MESSES.
O COLORS.
O SURPRISES
ALLOWED.
EVER.
978 1 4998 0277 1
BAR CODE STAMPER
978 1 4998 0277 1

Wait! Don't go any further! How did *color* get inside our perfectly clean factory?
Someone didn't follow the rules. Someone brought an outside mess into the Black and White Factory.
Could you help us? Use your fingers to wipe the color off the bar code. Go on, put some muscle into it!

Quick! Do something!
Rub the colors with your sleeve.
Or your elbow.
Something.

NO MESSES.
NO COLORS.
NO SURPRISES
ALLOWED
EVER.
We can't have any color in the Black and White Factory!

I've got an idea. Hold the book upright and tilt it so the color drips down the bottom of the page.

Nice job!
You made the color
drip out of the book.
The factory is
spotless again.

Uh-oh. Now there are more colors creeping in from all that tilting!
There's only one way to fix this. Swirl the book in a circle so the colors fly off the page.

We've got one more possible solution. Quick! Back to the top-secret Experiment Room.

If there's one thing that might be able to clean up our big, terrible mess, it's this machine.
AIR-POWERED COMPREHENSIVE CLEANING CONTRAPTION
NOZZLE
FOR EMERGENCIES ONLY. INSTRUCTIONS: BLOW AIR INTO THE NOZZLE TO START CONTRAPTION